The
Tiara
Club

at Emerald
Castle

For dearest Zoe –
with my love x
VF
With very special thanks to JD

ORCHARD BOOKS
338 Euston Road, London NW1 3BH
Orchard Books Australia
Level 17/207 Kent St, Sydney, NSW 2000

A Paperback Original
First published in Great Britain in 2008

A CIP catalogue record for this book is available
from the British Library.

ISBN 978 1 84616 874 1

1 3 5 7 9 10 8 6 4 2

Printed in Great Britain

The paper and board used in this paperback are natural recyclable products
made from wood grown in sustainable forests. The manufacturing processes
conform to the environmental regulations of the country of origin.

Orchard Books is a division of Hachette Children's Books,
an Hachette Livre UK company

www.hachettelivre.co.uk

The Tiara Club

at Emerald Castle

Princess Zoe

and the Wishing Shell

By Vivian French

ORCHARD BOOKS

The Royal Palace Academy
for the Preparation of Perfect Princesses

(Known to our students as "*The Princess Academy*")

OUR SCHOOL MOTTO:
*A Perfect Princess always thinks of others
before herself, and is kind, caring and truthful.*

**Emerald Castle offers a complete education for
Tiara Club princesses while taking full advantage of
our seaside situation. The curriculum includes:**

A visit to Emerald Sea World Aquarium and Education Pool	*Swimming lessons (safely supervised at all times)*
A visit to Seabird Island	*Whale watching*

**Our headteacher, Queen Gwendoline, is present at all
times, and students are well looked after by the school
Fairy Godmother, Fairy Angora.**

Our resident staff and visiting experts include:

QUEEN MOLLY (Sports and games)	*KING JONATHAN (Captain of the Royal Yacht)*
LORD HENRY (Natural History)	*QUEEN MOTHER MATILDA (Etiquette, Posture and Flower Arranging)*

We award tiara points to encourage our Tiara Club princesses towards the next level. All princesses who win enough points at Emerald Castle will be presented with their Emerald Sashes and attend a celebration ball.

Emerald Sash Tiara Club princesses are invited to return to Diamond Turrets, our superb residence for Perfect Princesses, where they may continue their education at a higher level.

PLEASE NOTE:
Princesses are expected to arrive at the Academy with a *minimum* of:

Twenty ballgowns
(with all necessary hoops, petticoats, etc)

Twelve day dresses

Seven gowns
suitable for garden parties, and other special day occasions

Twelve tiaras

Dancing shoes
five pairs

Velvet slippers
three pairs

Riding boots
two pairs

Swimming costumes, playsuits, parasols, sun hats and other essential outdoor accessories as required

Hi there - I am Princess Zoe,
and I'm SO pleased you're here with us at
Emerald Castle! I don't know about you, but
I find it REALLY hard to concentrate on
lessons when the sun is shining and the sea
is only moments away. I know Amelia, Leah,
Ruby, Millie and Rachel feel the same
way...oh! Have you met them yet? They
share Daffodil Room with me, and
we're all very best friends...

Chapter One

We usually have deportment lessons on Friday mornings, and it can be a bit scary as Queen Mother Matilda takes the class, and she's VERY fierce. As it was getting near the end of term we'd been practising for the Emerald Castle Presentation Day. We were all going to parade up and down the pier before we were given our sashes, and Queen Mother Matilda spent every lesson barking, "Walk for six steps, then TURN! DO try and be graceful, princesses!"

"I'm sure I'll be much too nervous to remember anything on the day," Rachel said gloomily as we walked towards the

ballroom. "I'm really scared I haven't got enough tiara points to win my sash."

"Me too," Amelia agreed.

"Don't even talk about it," I groaned. "The last time I tried to add up my points it came to about thirty, and Diamonde spent the whole of last week boasting that she had at least two hundred."

"Humph!" Ruby made a face. "I think it's a bit unlikely that she's got that many more than you, Zoe."

"That's right." Leah patted me on the back. "You've probably got LOADS more than her. Perhaps you just can't count!"

It was nice of my friends to be so supportive, but I really was feeling anxious. I'd had a couple of terrible dreams about being the only princess in the whole school who didn't get her Emerald Sash, and I couldn't help wondering if they might be the sort of dreams that came true...

"Look!" Amelia nudged me. "Fairy G's in the ballroom instead of Queen Mum Mattie! We can't be having deportment after all."

I looked round, and Amelia was right. Fairy G, our school fairy godmother, was standing on the platform at the end of the ballroom.

There were rows and rows of chairs and tables arranged as if we were going to have some kind of exam. My heart sank. I couldn't remember anyone saying anything about revision or preparation, but I knew I'd been spending a lot of time staring out of the window recently, and it was quite possible I hadn't written it down in my work book.

"Princesses – please sit down," Fairy G boomed. She really does have the LOUDEST voice, and we all scurried to our places. "Now," she went on, "I know you were expecting a deportment

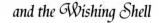

lesson, but there's a special end-of-term tradition here at Emerald Castle." She fished about in her huge black bag, and brought out a beautiful curly shell.

Carefully putting it on the table in front of her, she went on, "This wishing shell was given to us by a very generous sea fairy, many years ago. If you make a kind and thoughtful wish, that wish will come true!"

There was a buzz of excitement, and Fairy G smiled at us. "Put up your hands if you remember the lesson I gave you on How to Use Wishes Wisely!"

We all put up our hands, and Fairy G nodded. "Good," she said, and waved her wand. At once a piece of paper and a pretty silver pencil appeared in front of each of us.

"Now, please write down your wish. Queen Gwendoline has asked me to check them, as there will be an award of ten tiara points for the best wish. We'll meet again after lunch – and that's when you'll each be able to whisper to the shell, and see if your wish is granted!"

With that, Fairy G folded her arms, and settled herself on the edge of the table.

Chapter Two

I stared at my paper, and sucked the end of my pencil. We'd had our lesson on wishes when we first came to the Princess Academy, and I knew we were meant to be thoughtful and unselfish...but was there anything else? I sneaked a little sideways look at Amelia, and she was happily writing away.

Diamonde and Gruella were whispering to each other, but when Fairy G frowned at them they started scribbling madly. Leah saw me looking round, and she gave me a tiny wink – but I still couldn't think of a wish. I sighed, and put my hand up.

"Yes?" Fairy G came striding towards me.

"Please," I said, "I can't think of a wish at the moment...not a really good one."

To my surprise Fairy G looked pleased. "That's quite all right, Zoe," she told me. "I'd much rather you thought about it instead of writing the first thing that comes into your head. In a few minutes Queen Mother Matilda is going to take you all to the pier to practise for the parade, so come and tell me what your wish is when you get back."

"Thank you very much," I said gratefully, and Fairy G gave me one of her beaming smiles.

"In the meantime, you can collect everyone else's papers. I'll look at them while you're outside."

I walked round collecting the wishes, and as I came to the twins Diamonde sneered at me. "Teacher's pet!" she hissed. I pretended not to hear as I took her paper and put it on top of the pile, but my cheeks were still glowing as I put the wishes on Fairy G's desk. I think Fairy G noticed something had happened, but she didn't say anything, and a moment later Queen Mother Matilda came sweeping into the ballroom.

"Princesses!" she announced. "Today we're having a dress rehearsal! Please hurry to your rooms and put on your best dresses – the dresses you will wear for our special day. I shall expect you to be waiting in the front hall in precisely twenty minutes!"

Of course that made me almost forget Diamonde, and I joined my friends as we hurried up the stairs to Daffodil Room. Our dresses were hanging in our wardrobes waiting for Presentation Day, and it was SO exciting to put them on! We just had time for a quick twirl in front of the mirror before we zoomed back downstairs, and – I'm sorry if this sounds boastful! – I couldn't help thinking my dress really did look pretty.

When we got downstairs again, though, we saw the twins – and they didn't just look pretty. They looked MAGNIFICENT! Both of them wore the grandest dresses with long satin trains covered in pearls, and white satin gloves, and Diamonde was wearing the most amazingly sparkly diamond brooch. Gruella saw me looking at it, and she pouted.

"It's not fair, is it, Zoe? We're twins, so we should BOTH have a brooch, but Diamonde says SHE wants to wear it."

Diamonde frowned. "I TOLD you, Gruella – when I made my

wish I wished for you to have one exactly the same. It was very unselfish and kind of me, so DO stop whining!"

"Do you think we'll all have our wishes granted?" Millie asked.

"Really!" Diamonde looked SO superior. "Don't you know ANYTHING, Millie? Of course we will."

Gruella shook her head. "No, we won't – not if they're silly ones. Alice says her big sister told her to wish for something sensible, because the wishing shell doesn't grant people wishes if they want fluffy bunnies, or curly hair, or things like that."

"I wished there'd be a wonderful end-of-term party," Ruby said. "Do you think that's OK?"

Gruella looked pleased that, for once, she was the centre of attention and not Diamonde. "That's a really good wish," she said. "I wished that too—"

"WHAT?" Diamonde went a nasty shade of purple. "But you PROMISED, Gruella! You PROMISED you'd wish I had more tiara points than anyone else! You're MEAN, and I HATE you, and after lunch I'm going to ask Fairy G if I can have my wish back!" And she stormed out of the front door to where Queen Mother Matilda was waiting.

Chapter Three

Gruella made a face as Diamonde disappeared. "She should have let me wear Mummy's brooch," she said crossly, and then clapped her hand over her mouth. "OH! I said I wouldn't say! PLEASE don't tell her I told you! She'll be FURIOUS!"

Rachel raised her eyebrows.

"But why did your mum lend Diamonde a brooch, and not you, Gruella?"

Gruella shuffled her feet, and looked awkward. "Mummy didn't exactly lend it to her. Diamonde took it when Mummy wasn't there."

"OH!" Ruby sounded really shocked, and Gruella shrugged. "I did tell her not to, but she said it matched her tiara."

"It's a beautiful brooch," Amelia said slowly. "It must be VERY valuable."

Gruella nodded, but Queen Mother Matilda appeared in the

doorway before she could say anything else.

"Come along! What ARE you doing, princesses? We haven't got all day, you know!"

"Sorry, Your Majesty," Millie and Leah said together, and we hurried outside and down the path that led to the pier. Gruella hooked her train over her arm and came with us; for once she didn't seem to want to be with

Diamonde. As she walked beside me she whispered, "Mummy once told us that brooch was worth thousands and thousands of pounds! Do you think if Diamonde's wish comes true my one will be worth the same?"

"I don't know," I said. I was feeling a bit uncomfortable. If the brooch was worth so much money, then surely Diamonde shouldn't be wearing it at school? But I couldn't tell anyone – that would be SO sneaky.

"Erm…" I said. "Don't you think Diamonde should keep it somewhere safe?"

"Oh, it'll be OK," Gruella said cheerfully.

A few minutes later we were on the pier, and we didn't have time to think of anything except how to walk with our heads up and our backs straight. Queen Mother Matilda said we could smile (but not TOO much) and she made us count our steps until it was time to twirl at the end of the pier and come back again.

"One, two, three, four, five, six, TWIRL, Zoe!" she called out, and I did my best – but it wasn't good enough. Our teacher tut-tutted at me, and beckoned to Diamonde. "Diamonde, dear," she said, "PLEASE show Zoe how it should be done!"

Of course, that made Diamonde toss her hair and stick her nose RIGHT up in the air as she walked towards us. Her brooch was sparkling so brightly it almost hurt my eyes, and I wasn't surprised Gruella wanted one too.

"It'll be my pleasure, Your Majesty," Diamonde said smugly,

and she set off down the pier, her train trailing behind her.

"Zoe, you follow on behind Diamonde," Queen Mother Matilda instructed, and I did as I was told. At the end of the pier Diamonde did a perfect twirl, but as she came back towards me she suddenly swerved so I walked STRAIGHT into her – and she gave a massive shriek.

"OUCH!" she screamed. "OUCH! Zoe's trodden on my foot!" She sounded SO false – but a second later she let out a real screech. "My BROOCH! It's GONE!"

Chapter Four

I've never ever seen anyone go as pale as Diamonde did just then. She was totally white as she staggered against the side of the pier. Queen Mum Mattie came fussing towards us, and almost pushed me out of the way.

"Which foot is it, Diamonde, dear?" she asked.

"It's not my foot, it's my brooch," Diamonde wailed loudly. "It fell off, and I can't see it anywhere—"

Queen Mother Matilda stopped looking sympathetic. "That trumpery sparkly thing?" she said, and then she paused. "I HOPE, Diamonde, you aren't going to tell me that that was a REAL diamond brooch? You know the school rules. All items of extreme value MUST be registered with Queen Gwendoline at the beginning of term!"

Diamonde opened her mouth, and then closed it again, and I could almost see her mind racing as she decided what to say. "It...it wasn't real," she muttered.

"Well then – there's no harm

done," Queen Mother Matilda said briskly. "I'm sure you can find another. Now, if your foot is all right let's see you promenade one more time, because you did NOT walk in a straight line!"

Somehow Diamonde managed to get to the end of the pier and back, but she looked dreadful, and I actually began to feel just a little bit sorry for her. Amelia went next, and then all of Poppy Room – and when it was my turn again I had a good look for the brooch as I sailed up and down. I couldn't see any sign of it – but I did have a good idea.

The tide was right in – the waves were as far up the beach as they could go – and I thought that when it went out again we might find Diamonde's brooch on the sand underneath the pier.

When Queen Mum Mattie finally said we could go back to school I made sure I was in the

same group as the twins. They had to walk quite slowly because of their long satin trains, and gradually everyone else went on ahead...but I stayed to tell them about my plan. Before I could say anything, though, Diamonde gave me the MOST horrible look, and grabbed Gruella's arm.

"Come on," she hissed. "It's ALL Zoe's fault! We don't want to walk with HER!" And she swept up her train, hooked it over her other arm, and positively rushed away. I was left feeling really silly.

"What was all that about?" Rachel had come across from her group to walk beside me. "The twins look as if they're running a race!"

"I was trying to tell them they could look for the brooch when it's low tide," I told her, "but Diamonde wouldn't listen."

Rachel shook her head. "I don't want to be unprincessy and mean," she said, "but if Diamonde won't speak to you, you can't help her."

"I suppose so," I said slowly. I knew Rachel was right, but I couldn't help remembering

Diamonde's face when she realised she'd lost the brooch – she'd looked like a really, REALLY terrified little rabbit.

Chapter Five

We had to change back into our ordinary clothes when we got back to school, and as we hung up our dresses in Daffodil Room, Rachel told Amelia, Ruby, Millie and Leah about the twins not speaking to me. Leah and Amelia agreed with Rachel that they didn't deserve any more help, but

Ruby and Millie weren't so sure.

"Maybe Diamonde was horrid because she was feeling so guilty," Millie said. "She's going to get into TERRIBLE trouble when her mum finds out!"

"Why don't we go down to the beach after school?" Ruby suggested. "We could have a look. It would be fun if we found it!"

Amelia giggled. "We could give it to Gruella. She might look after it better!"

We agreed that we'd go for a walk on the beach that evening, then hurried down to lunch. Gruella was already sitting with Lisa from Lavender Room, but Diamonde came in after us, and I couldn't help noticing that her eyes were red as if she'd been crying. She went to sit by herself, and it was weird – I knew she'd been stupid and mean and horrible, but there was something about the way she was drooping over the table that made me feel really sorry for her. I hesitated for a minute, and glanced across to where all my friends were. They were chatting and laughing together, and when Ruby saw me looking she blew me a kiss and patted the seat beside her.

"I'm SO lucky!" I thought. "I've got SUCH brilliant friends. If I had a million ZILLION wishes I couldn't wish for anything better." Then I thought, "But Diamonde hasn't got any friends at all." And I really, REALLY didn't want to, but I made myself go and sit next to her. She looked up in surprise, and I half expected her to snap or sneer at me, but she didn't. She gave a huge sigh, and went on fiddling with her knife and fork.

"Diamonde," I said, "I still haven't chosen my wish. If I wished your brooch was safely on the sand under the pier, would you promise to take it straight to Queen Gwendoline, or Fairy G?"

There was a long pause, and then she nodded. "OK, then," I said, and I got up from the table and went to look for Fairy G before I changed my mind.

I was only halfway to the door when Fairy G came marching in. As soon as she saw me she pulled a piece of paper out of her bag. "Have you chosen your wish, Zoe?" she asked, and I said I had.

"Write it down," Fairy G said. "Quickly, now. We're going to bring in the wishing shell as soon as you've all finished eating your lunch!"

I scribbled down my wish, and Fairy G glanced at it. "I see," she said. "Hmm. That seems very generous to me, Zoe."

And then she stomped off to the other end of the dining hall to sit with Queen Gwendoline, and I went back to sit with Diamonde. She still didn't say anything...but a moment later when Amelia, Ruby, Millie, Rachel and Leah came to join us she gave me a watery smile.

"Thank you," she whispered.

Chapter Six

We'd just finished lunch when there was a fanfare of trumpets, and a page marched in with the wishing shell on a large velvet cushion. Fairy G stood up, and gave the shell a tap with her wand...and it glowed as if there was a bright pink light inside it.

"Please make a line!" Queen Gwendoline ordered, and we did as we were told – although we could hardly breathe for excitement. One by one we filed up to the shell and whispered our wish – and it was EXTRAORDINARY!

As soon as Amelia had had her turn the rest of us found we were wearing the most BEAUTIFUL necklaces...and when it was Millie's turn, Amelia had one too! And the dining hall was full of musicians, and decorations, and pages holding invitations to a fabulous end-of-term ball – and just as soon as Diamonde walked away from the wishing shell a brooch sparkled wonderfully on the front of Gruella's dress. Gruella gave a loud squeal, and flung her arms round her sister.

"THANK YOU! THANK YOU!" she said. "I'm so sorry I was cross."

"That's OK," Diamonde said, and then it was my turn. I walked up to the shell, and I whispered my wish...and for an awful moment I thought nothing would

happen. But then the shell gave a little extra glow – and I knew everything was going to be all right. Diamonde saw my face, and dashed up to Queen Gwendoline.

"Please," she said, and she curtsied very low, "please may I run down to the beach and look under the pier? I...I was very silly, and I took Mummy's best diamond brooch without asking, and it fell off my dress... but I think it might be on the sand..."

Queen Gwendoline looked at her, and frowned. "Did you ask for your brooch to be found, Diamonde? If so, I'm extremely surprised the wishing shell granted your wish."

Diamonde shook her head. "No, Your Majesty. Zoe wished for

me." She swallowed hard, and looked at me shyly. "She...she's a Perfect Princess."

Queen Gwendoline's face cleared, and she smiled. "You're quite right, Diamonde. Only a Perfect Princess would have wished to help someone in trouble. Run along and fetch your brooch, and we'll put it safely away in my study. Oh, and Zoe!"

"Yes, Your Majesty?" I said.

"Ten tiara points for the very best wish! And I don't think anyone will mind if I tell you that you now have more tiara points than any other princess, and I will be delighted to present you with your Emerald Sash on Presentation Day. You have CERTAINLY earned it!"

*

And that's exactly what happened.
Presentation Day was just
FABULOUS! We all wore the lovely

necklaces Amelia and Millie had wished for, and we paraded and twirled on the pier to perfection!

There was the most GLORIOUS ball afterwards; at least half of the princesses at Emerald Castle

had wished for that – although
I think there might have been
one anyway.

I can't wait until next term. Diamond Turrets!

And as long as all my friends are there, it'll be just perfect...

So make sure you're there too!

Don't miss  website at:

www.tiaraclub.co.uk

Keep up to date with the latest
Tiara Club books and meet all
your favourite princesses!

There is SO much to see and do,
including games and activities. You can
even become an exclusive member of the
Tiara Club Princess Academy.

PLUS, there's an exciting
Emerald Castle competition
with a truly AMAZING prize!

Be a Perfect Princess — check it out today!

This summer, look out for

Emerald Ball

ISBN: 978 1 84616 881 9

Two stories in one fabulous book!

Hello there – I'm Princess Leah, and it's
SO lovely to know you're here with us!
Don't you just adore Emerald Castle?
We do. Oh! I'm so sorry! You do know
the rest of Daffodil Room, don't you?
Amelia, Ruby, Zoe, Millie and Rachel – they're
my special friends, just like you. Actually,
most people at Emerald Castle are very
nice – it's only Diamonde and Gruella who
are mean and nasty...you just never
know what they're going to do next!

"We know something you don't know! We know something you don't know!"

We did our best to ignore Diamonde as she minced her way past us, arm in arm with Gruella, but it wasn't easy. She was obviously DYING for us to ask her what she was talking about. Once she reached the other side of the recreation room she made Gruella walk all the way back again, just so she could keep smiling her Know-It-All smile at us. In the end Millie couldn't bear it any longer.

"So what IS it you know and

we don't?" she asked.

Diamonde smoothed her hair back, and tried to look superior. "That's for you to find out!" She gave a silly giggle, and nudged Gruella. "It's something very, very special, isn't it, Gruella? And WE'RE going to win!"

Gruella nodded. "We're going to show Princess Beryl we're the best!"

"Who's Princess Beryl?" Ruby asked, but Diamonde shook her head. "It's a secret." And she giggled again in the most maddening way.

"Well," I said, "I don't really

care about your secret. I'm going to go and have a paddle. Is anyone else coming?"

Of course Amelia, Rachel, Millie, Zoe and Ruby said they'd come with me, and we all trooped out together.

~ *Want to read more?* ~
Emerald Ball is out in July 2008!